If They Only Knew

ANONNA REIGN

Library of Congress Control Number: 2025901697

ISBN
979-8-89641-037-9 (Paperback)
979-8-89641-038-6 (eBook)
979-8-89641-036-2 (Hardcover)

If They Only Knew

Table of Contents

Introduction ix

Chapter 1 1

Chapter 2 8

Chapter 3 15

Chapter 4 19

Chapter 5 25

Chapter 6 30

Chapter 7 35

Chapter 8 41

Chapter 9 44

Chapter 10 49

Chapter 11 54

Chapter 12 60

For He shall give His angels charge over you,
To keep you in all your ways.

Psalm 91:12

Introduction

"Taylor, did you get my dress from the cleaners?" "Yes mom," Taylor answered. "Did you set the table?" "Yes mother! Mom, everything is going to be fine. Stop worrying," Taylor said laughing. The last time she worried to this degree was when she met Taylor's stepdad for the first time. Taylor's brother Mike was coming home, and her mom wanted everything to be perfect.

Her mom adopted Mike at the age 4, after her sister died in a car crash. They always promised each other they would look after each other's kids if something happened to one of them, and Taylor's mom kept her promise after her sister passed away. Mom loved Mike as if he was her biological son, and she raised him into a good young man. Mike was just coming home from the army, and mom had prepared a big dinner to welcome him home.

"Welcome home Mike!" We all shouted when Mike got home.

"Hey," Mike said, as he grabbed our mother and hugged her.

"Is that you, Bug?" Mike said, referring to Taylor by her nickname. "I tell you it seems like you get prettier by the minute," Mike said, grabbing Taylor and hugging her.

Mike had a way of making you feel like the most beautiful girl in the world. Even though Taylor felt that beauty skipped her in the family. But not Mike, he was the spitting image of his mother. They had the same chestnut brown eyes, light brown skin, and a million-dollar smile that could win anybody's heart. Our stepfather, Steven, came home an hour late, just in time for dinner. When he saw Mike, he gave him a few punches to see how strong he had gotten. "All right, no playing around in my kitchen," Mom said, poking our stepdad in the chest. "Ok, Nora," Steven said, sitting down. "So, what are you planning to do, now that your home, Mike," Steven asked. "Well, I plan on getting a job, and if it's OK with my two wonderful parents, I wanted to stay here until I find me a place of my own," Mike said, hopefully. "Now you know you're always welcome here son," Steven said, giving Mike a playful shove.

After dinner Nora and Steven stayed behind to wash dishes, giving Taylor a chance to spend time with her brother. They sat on their old swings in the back yard. They spent most of their time back there when they were kids. "So, how is school?" Mike asked, breaking the silence. "It's terrible!" Taylor said. "What do you mean terrible? What's going on?" Mike asked. "Well for starters, nobody likes me." Taylor began. "They think that I'm too skinny, they call me ugly, and they say that I'm nerdy," Taylor whimpered. "What!" Mike said. "You better not believe any of those lies, Taylor. You are one of the prettiest girls that I know. The people that are spreading those lies are probably jealous. Don't pay them any attention," Mike said, wrapping his arms around his little sister. "Come on, Mike said, grabbing Taylor's arm. "I'm taking you for a drive." Steven came to the door when Mike was pulling out of the driveway and smiled and waved goodbye.

Mike pulled up at a park that he and Taylor went to all the time as kids. "So, how long have you had this car, Mike?" Taylor asked looking around. "This will be my 7th month," Mike said, relaxing his head on the back of his seat. "Man, I never been in a car this nice before, it has so many buttons, that I can hardly count them," Taylor gushed. "Well, that's what happens when you put God first, he blesses you not only with spiritual things but natural things as well." "God?!" Taylor said, surprised. "Yeah, being away from home so long almost killed me, Bug, I was around many people but was still all alone. But God was there every step of the way, that is why I put my trust in Jesus." Mike said. "That's deep," Taylor said, feeling a little uncomfortable. "I wish I could have the faith that you have, but I just… Oh my God," Taylor said, with a scared look on her face. Mike turned to see what had his sister's attention. It was a man in a black ski mask holding a gun up to Mike's window. "Get out of the car," the man said, trying not to sound scared. Mike turned to face his baby sister who was in tears. "It's going to be alright," Mike said, nodding his head for Taylor to take off her seatbelt. Taylor reached for her seat belt and slowly took it off. She opened the door, but she turned around and notice that Mike seat belt was stuck. Taylor tried to help Mike with his seat belt, but he pushed her. "Get out, Taylor!" Mike cried.

Mike knew that the man wasn't leaving without the car that he wanted so badly, that's why he was trying to get his sister out of the car. The man started getting impatient. "Get out of the car," he shouted. Not knowing that Mike couldn't get out. The man rage grew stronger, and he began shooting into the car.

1
CHAPTER

A few days later a lady named Lisa was sitting on the edge of her bed with a gun. She was crying as if her whole world was gone. In one hand, she held tight to a picture, that had a man and two kids on it. She kept saying, "It should've been me Lord, I was the one who should've died, God." Sweat poured off her head, as if she was in a sauna. She could hear a voice telling her not to do it. Was it all in her mind or were these voices real. The voice continued, "God loves you so much, Lisa, this is not the way to go." Lisa looked around, "Who's there?" she asked. "I can hear your voice, who are you?" Lisa asked. The angel looked at her and then turned to face another angel who was standing in the doorway. "Gabriel!" the angel said, looking surprised. "What are you doing here," the angel asked. Gabriel stood there with a smile on his face.

"I have a message for you, Anna, Gabriel began. "Our Lord has a new assignment for you," Gabriel announced. "OK., but what about…. "She will be fine," Gabriel said, interrupting Anna. "Look!" Gabriel said, pointing to the woman named Lisa. Lisa dropped her gun on the bed and began to pray. Anna smiled with great happiness. "You see Anna," Gabriel said smiling. "Your work here is done."

Gabriel brought Anna to a funeral. "What's going on?" Anna asked. "The boy in the casket name is Mike Nelson," Gabriel explained. "He was murdered a few days ago." "He was taking his sister out for a ride, when all of a sudden, a man with a gun came to steal his car and ended up taking the young man's life." "Oh no!" Anna said, putting her hands over her mouth. "Don't worry! Mike is with our Adonai," Gabriel said. "He will never experience pain ever again." "Well since he's with our Adonai already, what is my assignment?" Anna asked. "Right there," Gabriel said, pointing to a young girl that was sitting with her two parents. "Her name is Taylor Nelson. She was Mike's sister. Mike was the most important person in her life, and now she feels as though she has nothing," Gabriel said. "She thinks she's all alone. She doesn't know how much our Elohim loves her," Gabriel continued. Anna looked at Taylor with great compassion. She noticed that Taylor had her head down crying. Anna read Taylor's thoughts, and she was saying the same thing that the woman named

Lisa was saying. "It should've been me who should have died." "Why God, why did you have to take my brother, why did you take the only person in this world that understood me." "Why God, why!" Taylor thought.

Later that day, Taylor sat in her room. "Taylor, do you need anything?" Her mother asked, opening her bedroom door. "No mom," Taylor said, putting her head down. "Do you want to talk?" Nora continued. "No, mom, I'm fine," Taylor said, looking away. "Are you sure," Nora asked again. "Please, I just want to be alone, mom," Taylor said crying. Nora looked at her with deep compassion and nodded her head. She closed her daughter's bedroom door. Taylor locked her bedroom door when her mother closed the door. She slowly walked to her dresser and opened it. She moved her clothes to the side and pulled out a small box. When she opened the box, Anna's eyes grew wide. There in the box were some pills. Taylor stared at the pills and burst into tears. Anna knew exactly what the young girl was trying to do. Anna began talking to her. "Don't do it Taylor," Anna pleaded. "You have a lot to live for. Think about your mother and father, Taylor, they love you so much," Anna continued. Taylor looked around as if she was searching for the voice she heard. She brushed it off as being, just her imagination. She looked at the pills again and put them in the drawer.

Nora sat on the couch looking worried. "Nora, she is going to be OK" Steven said, while rubbing his wife's back. "She wasn't ready for something like this, Steven, Nora said. "I mean… Taylor is already having problems at school with the other kids, and now this." "How are we going to help her through this?" Nora asked. Steven held his wife in his arms, "I don't know how we're going to get through this, but we must trust God, Nora. God will get us through this, baby," Steven said. Steven got up from the couch. "I'm going to run you some bath water, I think it will help, if you would just relax for a while," Steven said. Nora looked at her husband and smiled. She got up and gave him a big hug. "What would I do without you?" Nora asked. "I don't know, probably go crazy," Steven said jokingly.

The next day, Taylor looked in the mirror one last time. She was wondering if going to school would be a mistake. "I have to go," she thought. Besides, being at home was making her crazy. She kept having nightmares about the night of the shooting. Sometimes she would even walk in on her mother crying. "Yes, it's time to go back. If my mother sees me trying to go on with my life, then maybe she will do the same." Taylor thought.

At breakfast, everyone ate quietly. No one really knew what to say. Anna sat there at the table as if she was a part of the family. She watched closely as Taylor tried to hide her tears behind her glasses. She tried smiling at her mom, but inside she wanted to scream. Anna decided that she couldn't take it anymore. "It's time I take it to the next level," Anna thought.

Taylor arrived at school around 9:00 o'clock. She wanted to get there late so she could avoid running into the varsity cheerleaders, who always made her life a living nightmare. When she saw one of the cheerleaders, Lucy Moore, standing in the hall, she went in the opposite direction. Lucy

looked up and saw Taylor. Normally she would have made fun of Taylor, but she was too busy talking to Caleb Anderson, the most popular boy at school. And there was no way that she was going to take her attention off Caleb Anderson.

Taylor made it around the corner and let out a sigh. She held her books up to her chest and darted down the hall again like a freight train. Suddenly, she ran into a girl who was walking towards her. The girl fell, dropping all of her books. "I'm so sorry," Taylor apologized. "I didn't see you," Taylor continued. "That's alright," the girl said, getting up. "I wasn't paying any attention either." The girl began helping Taylor pick up the books they'd dropped. Taylor looked at the girl and noticed right away that she had never seen her before. "She must be a new student," Taylor thought. The girl was beautiful. She had long beautiful locks that went down to her waste. She had perfect mahogany skin, and beautiful green eyes. She was definitely the prettiest girl she'd ever seen. She looked like she would fit in perfectly with the varsity cheerleaders. Taylor smiled when she imagined the look on Lucy's face when she discovered she was no longer the prettiest girl in the school.

"Is this your first day?" Taylor asked. "Is it that obvious?" the girl asked, with a laugh. "Yes!" Taylor smiled. "My name is, Taylor," Taylor said, holding out her hand. "My name is Anna," the girl said, shaking her hand. "Anna, that's a pretty name." "Thank you!" Anna said. "I was wondering could you show me to my class?" Anna asked. "Sure," Taylor said, excitedly. "What's your teacher's name?" "Let's see," Anna said, looking at her papers. "Mrs. Rogers is her name. "That's my teacher too," Taylor said, with a smile. Taylor and Anna walked to class together. Taylor was shocked at the fact that Anna wasn't ashamed to be seen with her. They arrived at the classroom. When they walked in all eyes were on Anna. Every boy in the class had their mouth wide open. The girls just looked at her with great envy. "Who is that," a girl asked one of the cheerleaders named Marcie? "I don't know," Marcie said. "Hi, my name is Anna," Anna said to the teacher. Mrs. Rogers looked at Anna with a confused look. "I wasn't told about a new student, there must be some mistake," Mrs. Roger said. She opened her book to see if Anna's name was in it. "I don't see your name," Mrs. Rogers said. With a simple nod of her head. Anna made her name appear in the teacher's book. "Are you sure," Anna asked? Mrs. Rogers looked again and there in plain sight was Anna's name. "Oh my, Mrs. Rogers said. "Here it is right here. I must need new glasses," she said laughing. "Well Anna, you can pick any seat that's empty," Mrs. Rogers said. Taylor and Anna went to be seated. Anna chose to sit next to Taylor. Anna could hear all the thoughts of the boys and girls around her. One boy was thinking "I got to get her number." Another boy was thinking. "Wait till Caleb see her." A girl over in the corner of the room was thinking. "What kind of conditioner does she use." Anna just smiled. "OK class we are going to go over the book that I told you to read over the weekend," Mrs. Rogers said. The kids all let out some kind of sigh.

"No need for the drama boys and girls, you had all weekend to get ready," Mrs. Rogers said. "I guess we will start with the character Keith," Mrs. Roger said, looking through her notes. "What was going through Keith's mind when he lost his best friend?" "I know, I know," a girl in the front of the class shouted. She was Brandy Smith. She was also the only friend Taylor had in the entire school. The other kids were looking at

Brandy with annoyance. "Yes Brandy," the teacher said. "The book said that he was feeling very lost to the point that he wanted to give up." Taylor's eyes began to get watery. The story that they were talking about reminded her of her own situation. She couldn't take it anymore. She got up and ran out of the classroom. Mrs. Rogers looked at Taylor run out and turn her attention back to the class as if she didn't care.

2

CHAPTER

Taylor ran through the halls of the school. She didn't stop until she made it to the girl's restroom. There in the restroom, she sat on one of the toilets as if she had to use it and cried. She became silent when she heard the restroom door open. It was Lucy and Mickey. Taylor remained silent. She didn't want them to know that she was in there. "Did you hear what happened to Mike Nelson?" Lucy asked, while combing her hair. "Yeah," Mickey said. "What a waste," Mickey said, while putting on a shade of pink lipstick. "I know right! I really thought that he would end up being my husband one day," Lucy said smiling. "Your husband, Mike was going to be mine," Mickey said, rolling her eyes. "Get serious, Mickey, do you really think that Mike would've picked you over me," Lucy said, standing there with her arms folded. "Oh, I know he would've picked me over you," Mickey said, with great confidence. "Mickey, no man can turn this down," Lucy boasted. "Mike and I should have been together, after all I am the pretties' girl in this town, and you only put the best with the best," Lucy said, fixing her hair. "I'm not going there with you, Lucy, the boy is dead," Mickey said, shaking her head. The restroom became silent.

"It's funny," Lucy said breaking the silence. "What?" Mickey asked. "How can a fine boy like Mike be some kin to a loser like Taylor?" Lucy asked with disgust. "Yeah, I've wondered the same thing," Mickey said laughing. "Did you see what she had on today?" Lucy asked. "No, what did she have on?" Mickey asked. "She had on these brown pants, looking like she just came from the good will." Mickey started laughing "You are so crazy girl," Mickey said. "Come on let's get to class before you get us both in trouble," Mickey said, while gently shoving her friend. "Me get in trouble. Girl, the only thing I have to do is pout, and Mrs. Jordan feels sorry for me, and will do whatever I want," Lucy confessed. Mickey shook her head and pushed Lucy out the door. Taylor just cried and cried. "How could they be so cruel," she thought. Just then, the door opened again. Taylor looked out of the crack of the door to see who it was. It was Anna. She stood there in the mirror fixing her makeup. Taylor watched Anna while she touched up her makeup. "I wish I was that pretty," Taylor thought. Anna could hear Taylor's thoughts. She slowly turned around. And Taylor jumped as if she'd seen a ghost. "Is someone there," Anna asked. Anna began to walk towards the stalls. Taylor had to think of something quick. "She will think I'm some kind of loser or something," Taylor thought. Taylor opened the door. "It's me, Taylor." "Oh, are you all right?" Anna asked. "Yes!" Taylor lied. "I just had to use the restroom." "OK., but if you need a friend to talk to, I'm here," Anna said. "Really?" Taylor asked. "Yes really," Anna said, with a warm smile. It was something about Anna's eyes that made Taylor trust her. "There is something about you that's different, I don't know what it is, but I feel like I can totally trust you," Taylor said. "You can trust me, Taylor." "Why are you being so nice to me," Taylor asked. "I mean you look like the type that would have nothing to do with a girl like me," Taylor continued. "Taylor, my father always taught me that it's not what's on the outside that matters, but what's on the inside," Anna explained. "So how about it, Anna said smiling, will you give me a chance to be a friend to you?" "Yeah!" Taylor said, with a smile.

Later that day, Lucy and her crew were sitting together at lunch. "Hey Lucy," Marcie began. "Rumors are… that you and Caleb are going steady." "Well, I don't want to brag, but he did ask me for my phone number," Lucy said, tossing her hair. "Really?" Marcie said. "Well, you better watch your back Lucy, because when he gets a look at the new girl, you might just be waiting by the phone," Marcie said, with a devilish look on her face. "What is that supposed to mean?" Lucy asked, with a frown on her face. "I'm just saying… there's a new girl here, and she looks like a goddess or something," Marcie admitted. "Oh, Marcie you are always imagining things. I'm sure this new girl doesn't look that good," Lucy said, with an arrogant look on her face. "Really, well I guess it's time for you to find out, because she's coming this way," Marcie said. Lucy looked at Marcie with a confused look and turned to see the new girl. Anna and Taylor walked in together as if they were best friends. Anna paid close attention to every word that came out of Taylor's mouth, as if what Taylor had to say was very important. "So where do you want to sit?" Anna asked. "How about right here," Taylor suggested. Anna and Taylor sat at the table that was next to the varsity cheerleader's table. "Don't look Anna but a girl named Lucy is looking at you like she seen a ghost," Taylor said laughing. Anna didn't look but she laughed at Taylor's expression of Lucy. "I don't get it. Why would a beautiful girl like that want to hang with Taylor," Mickey said confused

"Maybe it's her cousin," Marcie said. "Yeah, maybe she is," Mickey said, looking at Anna and Taylor. "Lucy, is there something wrong?" Marcie asked. "No! I'm just peachy. Where did she come from?" Lucy snapped. "Maybe she's from an island or something," Mickey said. "Well, I don't care where she came from, she is not going to mess things up with Caleb and me," Lucy said angrily.

Brandy walked up to the table where Anna and Taylor were sitting. "Anna this is Brandy," Taylor said. "Hi!" Brandy said, sitting down. "Hello," Anna said, with a warm smile. "Wow, you are so pretty," Brandy said, looking at Anna. "Thank you!" Anna said. "So, what are you doing tonight, Taylor?"

Brandy asked. "I don't know," Taylor admitted. "Well, I think you don't need to be alone right now. What do you think, Anna?" Brandy asked. "Oh, I agree," Anna said. "Well, what do you suppose I do?" Taylor asked. "How about I spend the night," Brandy suggested. "We can have something like a slumber party to cheer you up," Brandy continued. "I guess," Taylor said, as if she was unsure. "Can you come too, Anna?" Taylor asked, hopefully. "I mean, would you like to come, or do you think your parents will say no?" "I'm sure my father won't mind," Anna said smiling. "Well, I guess I'll see you guys tonight," Taylor said smiling.

Later that day Taylor arrived home looking tired. "How was your day?" Nora asked. "It was great, mom." Nora turned around looking surprised. She had never heard Taylor talk about school like that. "So, what happened?" Nora asked with a smile. "Well, I met a new friend today," Taylor said. "Really," Nora said, covering her mouth. "Mom, she is so nice," Taylor said. "I'm happy for you baby," Nora said, giving her a hug. "By the way mom, I was wondering if Brandy and my new friend can come over tonight? We wanted to have a sleep over." Taylor explained. "I think that's a great idea, with all the stress you've been under, a few friends coming over will probably do you some good. I'll help you set up everything," Nora said, with a smile. "Thanks mom! Taylor said, hugging her.

That night, Taylor waited patiently for Anna and Brandy to arrive. She wanted to make sure that everything looked perfect. "Will you stop," Steven said, gently hitting Taylor's hand. "Everything is perfect," he continued. Just then, the doorbell rang. "Oh, it's them," Taylor said, excitedly. Taylor opened the door, and there on the other side, stood Brandy. "Hey!" Brandy said, wiping her feet on the rug.

"Hi!" Taylor said. "Is Anna here yet?" Brandy asked. "No, she hasn't made it yet," Taylor said, trying not to sound disappointed. "Do you think she's really coming?" Brandy asked. "I sure hope so," Taylor said, looking out the window. "Come on Taylor, let's have some punch," Brandy said, getting some cups together. "OK" Taylor said," sitting down. "This is really good," Brandy said, licking her lips. The doorbell rang again. "It's her," Taylor said, getting excited. "I'll get it," Nora said, coming in. Nora opened the door and there standing in the door was Anna. "Hello!" Nora said. "You must be Anna." "Yes ma'am," Anna said. "I brought some cookies if that's OK." Anna said, coming in. "That's fine," Nora said. "They smell wonderful." Nora said, as she pulled a cookie out to taste one. She acted like she was going to fall out. "These are the best cookies I've ever tasted; you have to give me the recipe," Nora insisted. "Yes ma'am," Anna said laughing. "You have to excuse my mother she's on medicine right now," Taylor joked as Nora walked away. "I heard that!" Nora shouted behind. "Well, what do you guys want to do?" Taylor asked. "I know!" Brandy shouted. "We can talk about boys." Taylor shook her head and led the girls to her room.

There in Taylor's room, they sat talking about every boy in school. "You know Anna rumors says that you might have a chance with Caleb Anderson," Brandy said, while putting on lip gloss. "I'm not interested," Anna admitted. "You're not interested in the best-looking boy in school?" Brandy said, looking puzzled. "No, I look for more in a boy than just looks," Anna replied. "That's the way it supposed to be," Taylor agreed. "But now a days, people judge you on your outer appearance," Taylor said, looking frustrated. "I think Justin Harp is a pretty decent boy," Anna said. "What, you know Justin?" Brandy asked. "Let's just say I know someone who knows Justin very well," Anna gushed. "Really?" Taylor asked. "Yeah really! Justin Harp is a good boy," Anna said. "He is so cute. In my opinion, he is the best-looking boy in school," Taylor pointed out.

"Now that's a boy, I wouldn't mind getting with, but I'm sure that he wouldn't even look my way," Taylor said, putting her head down. "Well, you never know," Anna said, as if she knew some secret.

The next day, Taylor woke up with a big smile on her face. She looked over at Brandy who was sound asleep with cake still on her face. Taylor put her hands over her mouth, trying to keep from laughing. When Brandy fell asleep, Anna and Taylor mischievously decorated Brandy's face with cake. "She is going to kill us," Taylor thought. She turned to look at Anna who was already awake. "You're up already?" Taylor asked. "Yes," Anna said, with a smile. "You know, Brandy is going to kill us when she finds out what we did to her face," Taylor said. Anna looked at Brandy and started laughing. Taylor couldn't help but laugh too. "What's so funny?" Brandy asked, waking up. Anna and Taylor couldn't speak. "What is it?" Brandy asked again. She turned and faced a mirror.

"I am going to get you guys," Brandy screamed, chasing Anna and Taylor around the room. "It was Taylor's idea," Anna shouted. "You, squealer!" Taylor said, picking up a pillow hitting Anna with it. "Girls keep it down, it is too early in the morning," Nora said, while peeping through Taylor's door. "Sorry mom," Taylor said apologizing.

Later that day the girls got ready. Taylor could not believe how beautiful Anna looked. It was like watching a real live celebrity in her house. They were all excited. They were about to be dropped off at the mall. "Girls, are you ready?" Nora asked. "We'll be right down," Taylor yelled.

When the girls made it to the car, Nora wasted no time and made her way down the road. Anna watched the angels that were on traffic duty. Their duties consisted of making sure the people were safe. One of the angels was flying so fast that he ran into the back of a car and hit his head. Anna put her hand over her mouth to keep from laughing. Brandy looked over at Anna, confused as to what was funny, and Anna pretended she had to cough. When Nora pulled up to a red light, angels began flying past. "Hey Anna," some of the angels said, passing by. Anna tried to wave "hi" but she pretended to stretched her arm when she saw Brandy looking at her like she was weird.

At the mall, Taylor noticed that a lot of the kids from school were there. "This is so cool," Taylor bellowed. "Come on girls, let's do some shopping,"

Brandy said. The girls went all over the mall having fun. They went in all kinds of stores, trying on clothes and playing with toys.

Later, the girls went to a spot called Big Burgers. It was a fast-food restaurant that all the kids from school hung out at. "You guys just sit here. I'll get us some burgers," Taylor said smiling. Taylor left to go get the burgers, while Anna and Brandy stayed back at the table laughing and having fun. At a nearby table, sat Lucy, Mickey, and Marcie. "Hey Lucy, look who's coming," Marcie said. Lucy looked at Taylor and frowned. "What is she doing here?" Marcie sneered. "I don't know but that new girl is with her too," Mickey said, with a confused look on her face. Taylor could feel the varsity cheerleaders looking at her, but she pretended not to notice. Besides, she felt safe for some reason when Anna was around. Taylor hurried and got the food. She walked past Lucy's group with a smile on her face. She was beginning to enjoy the fact that Lucy was getting jealous of Anna. Taylor sat the food on the table. "Thank you," Anna said, grabbing her burger. "Don't look now Anna, but here comes Caleb and his crew. He's headed towards our table," Brandy said.

Caleb, Tyler, and Destin came to Taylor's table. "Hey Taylor," Caleb said, with a smile. "Hi!" Taylor said, trying not to sound too nerdy. She never had Caleb Anderson say hi to her before. "Well, are you going to introduce me to your friend?" Caleb said, looking at Anna. "Oh, this is my friend, Anna," Taylor said. "Hi!" Caleb said, reaching out his hand to shake Anna's hand. "Hello!" Anna said, shaking his hand. Taylor could sense that Caleb and his crew wanted to sit down to get to know Anna, so she asked them to join them at their table. "I don't believe it, Caleb is sitting with that loser," Lucy said, rolling her eyes. "Lucy, I know you are not going to just let that girl come in, and steal your man," Marcie said. Lucy looked at Marcie, and then back at Anna. "She will never get Caleb," Lucy said, with great confidence.

4
CHAPTER

Later that night Brandy had to go home. She promised her mother that she would help her brother with his science project. "Bye Anna, bye Taylor," Brandy said, leaving out. "Bye!" they both said waving. "Well, that was fun," Taylor said, putting her shopping bags on the bed. "I haven't had this much fun since…" Taylor put her head down, it was hard for her to talk about Mike. "Since what?" Anna asked. "Since my brother, Mike." We always did fun things like this. He was always there for me. Always helping me. But now he's gone, and I just don't know how I can make it without him," Taylor said, burying her face in her hands. "Why Anna! Why did he have to leave?" Taylor asked, with tears in her eyes. Anna looked at her with deep compassion. "Why does God just put wonderful people here and then just take them away." "Taylor, God send people here to fulfill their destiny, and when they have finished the work that they have down here, God takes them home to enjoy a life of peace," Anna said, touching her hand. Taylor gave Anna a forced smile. "You said that your brother was always there for you, right. And that he was always helping you. Maybe that was part of his assignment here on earth," Anna suggested. "You think so?" Taylor asked. "Yes, I think so," Anna said, rubbing Taylor's back. Taylor felt comfortable talking to Anna. They sat there all night talking about Mike and the kids at school.

"I can't believe that Caleb came to sit with us," Taylor said, shaking her head. "Did you see the look on Lucy's face?" Taylor asked. "Yes, I did, and she wasn't looking so happy," Anna observed. "Well Anna, you can't help it if you are the prettiest girl in school." "Yes, but I still want to make sure that I don't hurt anyone," Anna said. "Why should you care about hurting her, I mean she's always going around hurting people for no reason," Taylor argued. "That's because people like Lucy really need help. They feel like they have to do certain things to stay popular." "How do you know so much?" Taylor asked. "Let's just say, my father is a good teacher," Anna said smiling. "I would love to meet your father one day," Taylor said. "Well, one day you will," Anna said smiling.

A day later, Taylor arrived at school feeling good. She spent all night talking with Anna. Anna left her house about 11.00 that night after Taylor had fallen asleep. Taylor couldn't wait for Brandy and Anna, to see how her outfit looked on her. It was an outfit that Anna picked out for her at the mall. "Wait till they see me, they will be so happy," she thought. Taylor went to her locker to get her books, but when she looked around, she saw Lucy and her crew standing there. "So, if it isn't the world's biggest nerd," Lucy said laughing. "You thought you were pretty funny the other day, inviting Caleb to your table. Well, you better watch your back, because I am one girl that you don't want to mess with," Lucy argued. "Oh, and I see you have a new outfit on, well that outfit doesn't go with your ugly face," Lucy said laughing. Taylor could feel tears come down her face as the kids all started laughing at Lucy's remark. "What's so funny?" a familiar voice asked. It was Anna. Lucy looked at Anna and rolled her eyes. "I said what's so funny?" Anna repeated. Marcie waited for Lucy to answer Anna. "What's it to you?" Marcie said, with an evil grin. Anna walked up to Marcie and looked her in the eyes. "Don't start nothing you can't finish," Anna warned. Marcie looked at Anna with fear in her eyes and backed off. Lucy saw Marcie getting scared and came up to Anna as if she was about to hit her. Anna showed no sign of fear when Lucy jumped in her face. "If you want to keep that gorgeous face of yours, I suggest you stay out of this," Lucy said. "Lucy Moore, you do not want to mess with me," Anna said. "You sit here and make fun of a girl that doesn't bother anyone, but what if the tables were turned?" Anna asked.

"What if you were the one getting treated like dirt, how would you feel?" Anna continued. Lucy looked away as if she didn't want to hear the answer.

"I'll tell you how. You wouldn't feel good at all. Now if you want to keep your popularity, I suggest you leave Taylor alone," Anna said.

"Is that some kind of threat?" Lucy asked. "No, Anna said, it's a promise." Lucy looked at Taylor and then at Anna again and walked away.

"Wow, I've never seen anyone stand up to Lucy and her crew like that," Taylor said. "Well, that's not what's important right now. Are you OK, Taylor?" Anna asked, with a concerned look on her face. "I am now," Taylor said, with a smile. Taylor and Anna began to walk to class. "Taylor, you look beautiful," Anna said, with a smile. "You really think so?" Taylor asked. "Yes," Anna said smiling.

Later that afternoon the girls sat in P.E. together. Brandy was doing laps with the other kids, while Taylor and Anna sat there talking. "I really enjoyed the talk we had yesterday," Taylor said. "Me too," Anna agreed. "Did you guys hear about the modeling contest?" A girl named Joan asked, interrupting Anna's and Taylor's conversation. "What contest?" Anna asked. "There is a contest that all the pretty girls in school enter. The contest helps pay for the books we use, and not only that, the girl also that wins get 30,000 dollars' worth of cash and prizes. Plus, this year, the girl who wins get a chance to model with the top super models in the world, with a modeling contract to go with it." Anna and Taylor looked at each other as if they were getting excited. "So, do you want to sign up Anna?" Joan asked, tossing her hair. "No thank you," Anna said, getting up. "What? Why not?" Joan asked. "I mean everyone in school knows that you could win," Joan said. "I'm just not interested," Anna argued. "Excuse us Joan I need to have a word with my friend," Taylor said. Taylor gently took Anna's arm and pulled her to the other side of the room. "Are you crazy, Anna?" Taylor asked. "This is the chance of a lifetime for you," Taylor continued. "Yes but, she didn't even ask you if you wanted to be in this contest," Anna recalled. "I don't like the way they treat you," Anna complained. "Don't worry about me, I'll be fine," Taylor assured her. "I don't care if I didn't get asked. I mean you heard what she said, it is for all the pretty girls," Taylor pointed out. "Yes, and that means you too," Anna argued. "Get real Anna, I wouldn't stand a chance in the contest, but you do," Taylor said. That's not true, Taylor, you are beautiful inside and out. That's what matters," Anna replied. "I'll tell you what, if you really want me in this contest, you get in it with me," Anna suggested. "Oh, I don't think so," Taylor said, shaking her head. "I'm not getting in it unless you get in it with me," Anna said, folding her arms. "Well since you put it that way, I guess I have no choice but to get in it," Taylor surrendered. "Well, it's settled," Anna said, getting ready to walk away. "Wait!" Taylor said, grabbing Anna's arm.

"What if they make fun of me?" Taylor worried. "Don't worry, I'll take care of you," Anna assured her. Anna walked over to Joan who was still waiting for an answer. "OK, Joan I'll get in the contest on one condition," Anna said. "And what's that? Joan asked. "You let Taylor in too," Anna insisted. "Oh, Anna I don't know about that," Joan said, shaking her head. "Well then, I walk,"

Anna said, walking away. "OK, OK, she can enter, I mean it's not like she will win, but if that's what it will take to get you in, then I'll sacrifice," Joan said, shaking her head.

"What did she say?" Taylor asked, when Anna came back. "Well, I'm not sure, but I think she said, you're in," Anna yelled out. "Really? I can't believe it," Taylor said, looking shock. "Well believe it because you're in," Anna said smiling. "But what about my hair and the way that I look," Taylor worried. "Don't worry about that. When I get through with you, you are going to be the best-looking girl in the school." "It's going to take a miracle to make that happen," Taylor grumbled. "Well, It just so happens, that I'm a firm believer of miracles," Anna said, with a suspicious grin on her face.

5

CHAPTER

Lucy pasted back and forth. "Did you just say that Taylor was going to be in the contest?" Lucy asked. "Yes, I did," Joan said embarrassingly. Lucy looked at Marcie, and they both started laughing. "What did you do to get that nerd in the contest?" Lucy sneered. "Well, she got in because Anna wouldn't get in unless Taylor was in with her," Joan confessed. "What?" Lucy fumed. "You asked Anna to be in the contest? What is wrong with you?" Lucy shouted. "She is so gorgeous! If she gets in, we don't stand a chance," Marcie added. "Joan, I win this contest every year and I am not about to let someone else win," Lucy snapped. "If you have ruined my chances of winning, I will never forgive you," Lucy said, walking away. "Why did you betray Lucy, Joan?" Marcie asked. "Look, Marcie I didn't betray anyone. My job is to get beautiful girls around the school to be in the contest, and Anna happens to be one of those beautiful girls. I'm just doing my job," Joan argued. Marcie began to pout. She had a bad feeling about the contest.

A week later, Anna helped Taylor prepare for the contest. "Hold still," Anna said, while brushing Taylor's beautiful woolly hair. "OK," Taylor said smiling. "How do I look?" Taylor asked. "You will know in a minute," Anna said. "Now be still," Anna continued. After Anna fixed Taylor's hair, she applied her makeup. After she applied Taylor's make up, she used her power to give Taylor her final touch. Taylor could feel chills run through her body. "It's kind of cold in here," Taylor said, holding her arms. "I feel a draft coming in here from somewhere." "Stop worrying," Anna fussed. Brandy came in to see what her friends were up to. When she walked in, she couldn't believe her eyes. "Oh my!" Brandy said, with her mouth wide opened. "What's wrong?" Taylor asked. "Do I look that bad." Taylor worried. "No, you look beautiful," Brandy said excitedly. Taylor looked at Brandy with a puzzled look, and then got up to look at herself in the mirror. Taylor couldn't believe her eyes. Her hair was long and beautiful. Her makeup was flawless. "I can't believe it Anna," Taylor cried. "I look like a model, Anna. Am I'm dreaming?" Taylor asked. She began to cry. "You're not dreaming, Taylor "You are awake," Anna said, with tears in her eyes. "I can't believe this," Taylor said, crying. "Thank you, Anna! Thank you so much." Taylor said, hugging her. "How can I ever repay you?" Taylor asked. "You can pay me by doing this for someone else. And to remember that true beauty comes from within," Anna said smiling. Taylor didn't understand what Anna was saying, so she just threw her arms around her again. "Hey, don't leave me out," Brandy shouted. They both started laughing and grabbed Brandy in for a hug too.

Later that day, Taylor practiced walking in heels. "This is hard," Taylor argued. "Just concentrate," Anna said. While Taylor wasn't looking, Anna used her powers to help her balance. "Hey, I think I'm getting it," Taylor laughed. "Yes, you got it all right," Brandy said, shaking her head. "If you walk any more sophisticated, you'll be up there with Jane Lacy," Brandy continued. Taylor and Brandy started laughing. Jane Lacy was one of the teachers who used to work at their school. She was always remembered for the way she walked. "So, what's next?" Taylor asked. "Well, we go shopping." Anna suggested. "That's good because I don't think my new look goes with these clothes," Taylor grumbled.

The girls headed down the stairs. "Hey mom, we are going to the mall," Taylor said. Nora turned to face her daughter and jumped as if she had seen a ghost. "Taylor baby, what happened to you?" Nora asked. Anna fixed my hair and gave me a makeover. "Baby you look beautiful," Nora said, giving Taylor a hug. "I got to hand it to you Anna, you have anointed hands! She looks like a different person," Nora exclaimed, with tears in her eyes. "I can't get all the credit Mrs. Nelson. Your daughter is naturally beautiful,"

Anna pointed out. "I can't argue with you on that," Nora said laughing. "OK, enough talk mom we have to go and get me an outfit for the contest," Taylor cut in. "What contest?" Nora asked. "It's a modeling contest at our school mom, and yours truly is in it." "When did this happen?" Nora asked. "The other day, Anna stood up for me and told Joan Miller, that she is not going to be in the contest unless they let me in," Taylor explained. "Really! Anna that was very thoughtful of you." "Thanks Mrs. Nelson," Anna said blushing. "Well, bye mom, we have to go," Taylor said, grabbing Anna's arm and heading out the door. "OK," Nora said, waving goodbye. What's going on?" Steven asked, walking in. "And was that our daughter that just ran past me?" "Yes! That was our daughter, she has turn into a little butterfly before our eyes." "Wow! She puts a new meaning to the phrase "Taylor-made" Steven said laughing. Nora started to laugh as well.

Taylor and Anna arrived at the mall around 5:00 o'clock p.m. They dropped Brandy off at the pizza gallery, where she was filling in as a waitress for her family. Brandy hated leaving Taylor with all the excitement going on, but her parents needed help trying to cook and serve the customers. "I think that looks perfect," Anna said, when Taylor came out of the dressing room. "You really think so?" Taylor asked. "Yes," Anna said. "Well, I'm going to keep it," Taylor blushed. Taylor and Anna shopped for an hour. They both got tired, so they decided to go to Big Burgers. They both sat there laughing and having fun. Taylor and Anna both looked like movie stars and some of the students stared at them in admiration.

Lucy and her crew sat at the next table. They seemed to be enjoying themselves, until they noticed that Anna was sitting across from them. "What is she doing here?" Marcie asked, with a frown. "Who is that with her?" Mickey asked. "I don't know, maybe it's her sister," Lucy guessed. "Don't look, but we are being watched," Anna said laughing. "By whom?" Taylor asked. "Lucy and her crew," Anna said. Taylor turned around and looked at Lucy. She was looking at Taylor as if she didn't know who she was. "Anna, do you think they know it's me?" Taylor asked. "No, they have no idea who you are," Anna said, sounding sure of herself. "Wow, this is great," Taylor said smiling. "Maybe I should go over there and let them know that it's me." Taylor said, getting up. "No, not right now," Anna warned. "They will know soon enough." Just then, Anna had a vision. She had a weird look on her face as if she'd seen a ghost. "Anna, are you alright?" Taylor asked. "Anna!" Taylor said, again waving her hand in her face. "I have to go," Anna said, getting up. "But Anna you haven't finished your burger," Taylor said, trying to stop her. But Anna was already headed for the door.

6
CHAPTER

Anna arrived at the pizza gallery in the form of an angel, where no one could see her. There on the floor lay Brandy. She was lying on the floor dying. People were gathered all around her trying to find out what was going on. Her mother was kneeling beside her crying. "Out of the way!" the paramedic said, trying to get through the crowd. "What happened?" one of the paramedics asked Brandy's mother as he knelt down to check Brandy to see if she was breathing. "She had an asthma attack," her mother said crying. The paramedic listened for a pause but couldn't find one. She's not breathing, he said, to the other paramedic that just walked in. Brandy's mother began to cry again, watching the paramedic do CPR on her daughter. Anna saw the devil had come to take Brandy. "What do you think you're doing?" Anna asked. "I'm coming to collect her soul," the devil said. "You're not touching one string of hair on her head," Anna said, getting in the devil's face. "Why not, Anna? She belongs to me," the devil argued. Brandy could see Anna and the devil arguing over her. "Anna!" she said. Anna looked at Brandy's soul and then back at the devil. "The Lord Jesus commands you to let her go," Anna shouted. When she said those words, the devil got powerless and disappeared. Brandy began to breathe again, and her soul returned to her body. "Brandy," her mother said, looking into her daughter's eyes. "Mom," Brandy said, looking scared. After Brandy gained consciousness, the paramedics took her to a nearby hospital.

"You are very lucky to still be with us," the nurse said, at the hospital. "Do you need anything?" the nurse continued. "No," Brandy said, shaking her head. Brandy's parents left to get some coffee from the hospital cafeteria. When Mrs. Smith looked up, she saw Taylor and Anna. "Is she alright?" Taylor asked. "Yes!" Mrs. Smith said, with a smile. "She is going to be just fine, you can go see her, she's in room 357," Mrs. Smith said.

"Thank you!" Taylor said.

Taylor and Anna went into the room with Brandy. "Hey girl! Taylor said, coming in. "Hi!" Brandy said, as if she was exhausted. Taylor went over to Brandy's bed and sat down beside her. Anna walked over to a chair that was near the bed and sat down. Anna noticed how Brandy looked at her in a weird way. "Brandy, what happened?" Taylor asked, breaking her focus. "I was standing at the table waiting for this couple's order, when all of sudden, I had an asthma attack. I collapsed on the floor, and well I can't remember too much after that," Brandy recalled. "But I do remember one thing," Brandy said, with a confused look on her face. "I saw this angel, and she looked just like you, Anna." "You must've really hit your head hard," Taylor said laughing. Anna tried to laugh too, but she knew that Brandy knew her secret. "Yeah, maybe so," Brandy said, looking Anna in the eyes. Anna turned away. She could read Brandy's thoughts. "I know what I saw," Brandy said, in her mind. "Taylor, could you let me talk to Anna alone?" Brandy asked. "Oh sure," Taylor said, getting up. Taylor gave Brandy a kiss on the forehead and left. "Brandy, I know what you're going to say," Anna said. "I'm sure you do, being that you're not from this world." Brandy replied. "Brandy please listen to me," Anna pleaded. She sat on Brandy's hospital bed. "What you think you know, it is better that you keep between us," Anna warned. "Why should I, Anna? Why should I keep your secret?" Brandy asked. "Because, Taylor doesn't need to know right now, trust me she won't understand." "She won't understand huh! Well help me to understand, Anna. Why are you here in the first place. Or better yet, tell me how long you were planning on keeping this secret from us," Brandy asked, in a bitter tone. "I'm here because Taylor is my assignment," Anna began. "Believe me, when I tell you that it was best that I kept my identity a secret. Brandy sometimes it's hard to figure out God's purpose. What I mean to say is… I don't understand why he allowed you to see me, but I do know that his purpose is always perfect," Anna assured her. "God loves his creation so much, that he sends angels like me to protect you," Anna explained. "So, after you help Taylor, then what? Do you just leave us?" Brandy asked. "Do you just walk away, Anna?" Brandy continued. Anna put her head down. "You are, aren't you? You're going away. How could this possibly help Taylor?" Brandy protested. "Brandy, Taylor is going to be fine" Anna assured her. "I don't know about that, Anna. "First, she loses Mike and now you. How is she going to survive this?" Brandy asked. "I'll tell you how, she has you and she has God watching over her. So please Brandy, don't tell her. I will tell Taylor everything, after the contest," Anna pleaded.

"Alright, Anna, but you better tell her," Brandy said. "Thank you so much," Anna said, with much gratitude. Anna started for the door. "Wait Anna!" Brandy said, stopping her at the door. Anna turned around to see what it was that Brandy wanted. "What is it, Brandy?" Anna asked. "Was that evil devil really going to take my soul?" Brandy asked. "Yes, Brandy I'm afraid so," Anna admitted. "Why Anna? I'm a good person. I make the honor roll every year. I obey my parents and never get into any trouble," Bandy said crying. "Well because you have not yet excepted Jesus into your heart," Anna said. "But I always thought that was just a made-up story," Brandy responded. "No, Brandy, it's not some made-up story. That's what the enemy wants you to believe. God is very real, Brandy." Brandy looked at Anna with tears in her eyes. "Anna, could you tell God that I'm sorry for not believing in him," Brandy said, between sobs. "He already knows you're sorry. "He's waiting right now for you to receive him into your heart," Anna said smiling. Brandy then said a prayer and asked Jesus to come into her heart. Anna started rejoicing. "Brandy, Heaven is rejoicing right now because of you," Anna said, holding her hand.

The next day Taylor was on her way to school. "I'm so nervous," she thought. This was her first day back at school since her new look. "I wish Anna was here," Taylor said to herself. Just then, Anna appeared. "Hey, I didn't even see you come up," Taylor said. "Are you ready?" Anna asked. "As ready as I'm going to get," Taylor mumbled. "Don't worry, you'll be fine," Anna said, grabbing Taylor's arm. When they walked into the school. Kids were staring at them. "That's it, I'm leaving," Taylor panicked. "Taylor, will you chill out, they are looking at you because you are beautiful, and because they don't know who you are," Anna said, trying to convince her. "Oh, well alright, this is going to be a lot of fun," Taylor said, with a devilish smile.

Taylor felt herself blush when she saw how all the popular boys were looking at her. She could see everyone whispering. "I wish I knew what they were saying," Taylor thought.

"Hey Lucy, isn't that the girl we saw last night?" Mickey asked. "Yeah, that's her," Lucy said. "What is she doing at our school?" Marcie asked. "I don't know but I hope she's not a new student," Lucy admitted. Just then, the bell rung and all the students started running, trying to get to their classes. "It's time," Anna said. "Time for everyone to know that it's you." "I'm ready," Taylor said exhaling.

Taylor and Anna arrived at their classroom. Anna went to take her seat. But Taylor was stopped by Mrs. Rogers. "May I help you?" Mrs. Rogers asked. Taylor looked at Mrs. Rogers with a confused look. "Excuse me," Taylor said. "You're new, right?" Mrs. Rogers asked. "No, Mrs. Rogers." Taylor said, feeling a little embarrassed. Taylor could feel her neck stiffen. Mrs. Rogers had no clue who she was. "It's me, Taylor," Taylor said, letting her secret out. The class all looked at Taylor in shock. "Is that really Taylor," they all asked themselves. "Why Taylor you look beautiful," Mrs. Rogers said smiling. "Thank you." Taylor began blushing. "You make sure that you get me an appointment with the one that did your makeover," Mrs. Rogers said jokingly. Taylor took her seat. She could see how everyone was looking at her in shock. "I don't believe this," Marcie said. "That's Taylor?" "Wow, talk about a full transformation," Mickey sighed. "And what's worse is, you guys are going to have to compete against her in the contest," Mickey continued. "Who knew, up under all that braided hair, was soft long curly hair, and without those bifocals… big beautiful brown eyes." "I think I'm going to be sick Mickey said, banging her head on her desk." "Will you stop Mickey! This is Taylor, the nerd you're talking about. Taylor is still a nobody, she can barely carry her schoolbooks, so how in the world do you think she's going to make it down the runway," Marcie sneered. "I hope your right, because I would hate to see you and Lucy lose to the biggest nerd in school." "Don't worry, I will do whatever I have to… to see that me or Lucy win that contest," Marcie said, with an evil look.

Later that day Taylor and Anna walked to the gym. The kids were already there, hanging up decorations for the modeling contest. "Wow, it looks great in here," Taylor said. "I'm so nervous, Anna," Taylor continued. "Don't be, you look beautiful. Besides, I'm with you every step of the way," Anna assured her. "I don't know what I would've done if you weren't here by my side," Taylor cried. "Hey, don't get all mushy on me. You're going to ruin your makeup," Anna said, wiping the tears from Taylor's face. Taylor and Anna walked to a girl sitting at a desk. Some of the girls were grabbing forms from off her desk. "How may I help you?" She asked. "Hi," Taylor said. "We are in the modeling contest," Taylor said, pointing to herself and Anna. "OK you have to fill out these forms," the girl said, giving Taylor and Anna some forms to fill out. "Thank you," Taylor said, walking away. Taylor and Anna went to be seated, so they could fill out their forms. "This is a lot to fill out," Anna said looking through her papers. "Yeah, look at question number 22. It asks if you ever had plastic surgery before," Taylor said, shaking her head.

"OK girls, I want everyone in the contest to come over here," a lady named Linda said. "Even if you're not through with your forms, please come," Linda continued. The girls all got up from where they were sitting and joined Linda sitting in a circle. "Hello, young ladies. If you don't know, my name is Mrs. Linda, and I'm over this year's modeling contest." The girls began cheering, and Mrs. Linda bowed her head in gratitude. "As some of you may know, this is my assistance, Joan." Joan got up and waved, so that the girls would know who she was. The girls began cheering for Joan, and Joan began to blush.

"Well, this year's contest is very exciting. It's much more exciting than the contests we've had in the past. This year the winner wins $30,000 dollars' worth of cash and prizes, and not only that, this year, the winner gets a chance to model with the top super models in the world. Isn't that great?" Mrs. Linda asked. The girls all let out a scream. "Now we won't know who the judges are, until the day of the contest, and the reason for that is so those of you with rich parents won't be trying to bribe the judges," Mrs. Linda said, giving some of the rich girls known for their bribery, a stern look. "Yes, that's right ladies, this year will be a fair contest. So, for those of you thinking about cheating, don't, because if you get caught, you are out," Mrs. Linda warned. "After the contest, we are having a dance, to celebrate the winner's victory. The winner gets to choose a date of her choice to be with. This year's chaperones are Destin

Tucker." The girls all screamed as Destin entered the gym, wearing a Nike gym suit. Mrs. Linda continued calling names. "Tyler Bradley." The girls kept screaming. Tyler came out and bowed down before the girls. Marcie grabbed one of Tyler's legs. "Ok, that's enough, Marcie" Mrs. Linda said, with a concerned look on her face. "Next we have Justin Harp," the girls started screaming again. Justin came out waving. "And last but not least, Caleb Anderson." Mrs. Linda could barely get his name out. The girls started jumping up and down and screaming to the top of their lungs. Caleb came out, and a lot of screaming girls ran after him. Taylor and Anna stayed behind looking annoyed. Mrs. Linda shook her head in grief.

"Ladies could you please come back, and Marcie, for the love of God give Caleb his hat back," Mrs. Linda said, with a frustrating sigh.

The girls all came running back and sat down. "That will be all boys," Mrs. Linda said, shaking her head. "Ok girls let me get your names to see if everyone is present." "Manny Brook." "Here," she said, raising her hand. "Amanda Rose. "Present," Amanda said. "Teresa Black." "Right here Mrs. Linda," Teresa said, waving her hand. "Lucy Moore." "Present," Lucy said, with a proud look on her face. "Ok, I see you, Lucy," Mrs. Linda said, annoyed by her arrogance. "Marcie Henderson." "Here," Marcie said. "Sarah Meyers. "Here." Sarah said. "Anna Jones." "Here," Anna said, with a smile. "And last but not lease, "Taylor Nelson." "Here," Taylor said, raising her hand. "Taylor," Mrs. Linda said in shock. "Yes Mrs. Linda." "You look wonderful," Mrs. Linda said. "Thank you," Taylor said blushing. "Oh, I think I'm going to be sick," Lucy whispered. Taylor looked at Lucy and rolled her eyes. "Ok girls, I want you to finish filling out your forms and the sheet attached to it, I want you to keep it, and make sure you read all of it. Because it has all the rules and requirements on there." All the girls sat there quietly filling out their forms. Taylor looked around, wondering if she belonged, if being there was a mistake.

8

CHAPTER

can't believe how different Taylor looks," Lucy fussed. "I mean for years she's the school's nerd. And now she's looking like one of us. How do you explain something like that?" Lucy went on. "A miracle?" Marcie asked. "A miracle my butt, something fishy is going on, and it is up to us to find out what that thing is," Lucy declared. "Maybe she's taking some kind of vitamins or something," Mickey suggested. "Mickey, vitamins don't have you looking like a goddess in a week." Lucy pointed out. "Look at her hair, and that body. Where did it come from. No, I tell you ladies something stinks. And I'm going to find out what it is," Lucy said. "You are just making a big deal over nothing," Mickey said. "So, the girl had a little luck, what's wrong with that?" Mickey continued. "Luck my foot, I'm telling you guys something is not right," Lucy argued.

"Hey Brandy," Taylor said, visiting Brandy one afternoon. "What's up?" Brandy said, hugging her friend. "I'm so glad your home," Taylor said. "I'm glad to be home. The hospital smells like old clothes, and don't let me mention the food," Brandy said laughing. "So, what's new?" Brandy asked, sitting down. "Well," Taylor began. "I'm officially in the contest. Lucy almost died," Taylor said laughing. Brandy started laughing too. "Man, I wish that I could've been there to see that," Brandy said, shaking her head. "There is something that I don't understand though," Taylor said confused. "At the last minute, Anna dropped out of the contest." Brandy got up turning around so that Taylor wouldn't see the weird look on her face. "Did she say why she got out of the contest?" Brandy asked. "No, she just said that I would understand later."

"She didn't tell you anything, did she?" Taylor asked. Brandy looked at Taylor, not sure of what to say. "Taylor, I don't know how to tell you this but…. "Hey you!" Anna said, interrupting Brandy. Brandy was shocked to see Anna standing there at her door. "Anna, we were just talking about you," Taylor said. "Really, well Taylor you have no time to talk, you better be getting ready for the big night." "Okay," Taylor said. She turned to Brandy and gave her a big hug. "I'll see you later," Taylor said. "Sure," Brandy said smiling. "Bye Anna!" "Bye Taylor, I'll be there in a little while." "OK," Taylor said, walking out of the door. "What are you doing, Brandy? You were going to tell her,"

Anna argued. "Anna, I don't like keeping my friend in the dark. I mean I feel like I'm lying to her." "Brandy you are not lying to her. There are just some things that friends don't tell each other," Anna reasoned. "Well not me, I tell Taylor everything." Brandy snapped. "Not everything, Brandy," Anna said. "Yes everything," Brandy continued. "Well, if you tell Taylor everything. Why didn't you tell her about the time you got expelled for drinking alcohol, or maybe you told her about the time you secretly voted for Lucy for class president instead of her. Brandy's mouth hung wide open. She couldn't believe Anna knew all of her dark secrets. "Okay you made your point. Will you stop doing that. I will admit that there are some things that we haven't discussed. But this will break her heart, if she has any idea that I knew about this." "Please believe me Brandy, when I say that everything will be fine. Believe me I know," Anna said, comforting her. "I guess you do know more than me. But for the record, Taylor always looked up to me, and I knew if I had told her about me getting expelled, it would change the way she looked at me," Brandy confessed. "Believe me Brandy when I say that Taylor won't look at you any different," Anna said smiling. "Really!" Brandy said hopefully. "You mean I've been carrying around this burden all this time and she wouldn't have looked down on me?" Brandy asked. Anna shook her head "no." "Wow, this is wonderful! Thank you, Anna," Brandy said, wrapping her arms around her. "You are so welcome," Anna said.

Later that day Taylor sat in the locker room getting ready for the contest. "Where is Anna?" She thought. She pasted the floor, wondering if she looked ok. "Hey!" a voice coming from the door said. It was Anna. "Hi," Taylor said relieved. "Are you ready for your big night? Anna asked. "I guess," Taylor said. "How do I look?" Taylor asked, spinning around. "You look absolutely beautiful," Anna said. Just then, Lucy and her crew came in. "Hey Taylor, were did you get that dress it is so pretty?" Lucy asked. Taylor looked at Anna with a surprised look. Lucy had never given her a compliment before. "Thank you, I got it from Fashion Less." "Oh, that's so nice." Lucy continued. "Oops," Lucy said, spilling her coffee on Taylor's dress. "Taylor I am so sorry, I tell you sometimes I can be so clumsy," Lucy said laughing. Marcie and Mickey began laughing as well. Taylor looked down at her dress and began to cry when she saw the huge stain on her dress. She looked at Lucy and her crew with tears in her eyes and ran out. Anna looked at Lucy with anger in her eyes. "What?" Lucy asked. "It was an accident, alright" Lucy lied. But Anna knew better. "So, Lucy, you said that sometimes you are a little clumsy huh?" Anna asked. Lucy looked at Marcie and Mickey with a confused look. "Yeah, I guess I do get a little clumsy," Lucy said. "Well Lucy clumsy is what you spoke and clumsy is what you will be," Anna said, walking out. "What was that all about Marcie asked. "I don't know, Lucy," admitted. "That was weird," Mickey added. "Girls forget Anna, she's just trying to scare us," Lucy assured them. Just then, Lucy turned to walk out and tripped over some books that were nearby. "Are you OK, Lucy?" Mickey asked, helping her up. "Yes! Lucy said. But every time she tried to get up, she would fall again. "Are you drunk?" Marcie asked. "No! Lucy snapped. Maybe it's those high heel shoes you're wearing," Marcie suggested. "It is not my shoes," Lucy fumed. "I know what it is, Anna she put a curse on me." "What?" Marcie asked. "I'm telling you she did this," Lucy fussed. "Lucy, Anna did not put a curse on you," Mickey said, laughing at the idea. "Think about it Mickey, right after she said those horrible things to me, I became very clumsy," Lucy explained. "I don't believe that, Lucy. Maybe you are just having a little bad luck. I mean everybody has a little bad luck," Mickey said. "Yeah Lucy, you said so yourself that Anna was just trying to scare us," Marcie agreed.

"Are you alright Taylor?" Anna asked walking in. "No, what I'm I going to do about this stain on my dress?" Taylor cried. "Oh, I can get that off," Anna said. Anna sat down next to Taylor and began to wipe her dress with some club soda. Just when Taylor wasn't looking, Anna used some of her powers to remove the stain. Taylor looked down at her dress. "Wow, Anna you got the stain out. I can't believe it! It's gone," Taylor said, hugging her. Just then, Mrs. Linda came in interrupting the girls. "It's time Taylor," Mrs. Linda said smiling. "Well, Taylor said, turning to Anna, this is it." "Don't worry, you are going to be fine," Anna said, giving Taylor a comforting hug. Taylor went to the door and looked back again. She knew that she could do it because Anna taught her to believe in God and in herself.

In the auditorium, Brandy sat in the audience waiting for the show to begin. "Hey! A voice behind Brandy said. "Oh, hey Anna," Brandy said, with a smile. "You're just in time, the show is about to begin," Brandy said. Mrs. Linda came out to a stage that looked like a runway stage. "Good evening," Mrs. Linda said, with a smile. "Welcome to the 2024 modeling competition. "This year is going to be our best year ever. Before we get started, I want to take time out to acknowledge our judges. This year we have from Glamour magazine, Karen Bell." Karen got up and turned to wave at the audience. "Next, we have the publisher of the book, 'Men Got To Be From Mars,' and former Supermodel Kirsty Brooks." Kirsty stood after her name was called and waved and blew kisses to the screaming males. "Last we have actor, Tom Brian." The audience all went wild as Tom got up and waved. "OK, let's give our judges another round of applause." The audience all started clapping and screaming, making the judges feel welcomed. "All right, lets meet this year's escorts." Mrs. Linda began calling out names. "Tyler Bradley, Destin Tucker, Justin Harp, and Caleb Anderson." The audience all started to cheer. "Thank you, boys," Mrs. Linda said, waving at the boys, as they all left the stage.

"OK, are you ready to meet this year's contestant?" The audience let out a big scream. "Ok first we have Sarah Meyers." Sarah came out with a beautiful gown on. She went down the runway and made beautiful turns. "Thank you, Sarah," Mrs. Linda said, as Sarah took her place on the stage. "Next coming to the stage, we have Teresa Black." Teresa came out and modeled her beautiful dress, and then stood next to Sarah. Mrs. Linda started back calling names. "Amanda Rose." Amanda came out and graced the stage with her beauty. "Marcie Henderson." Marcie came out and modeled her dress. "Manny Brook." Manny came out with a sassy walk and took her place next to the other girls. "Lucy Moore." Lucy came out with a proud look on her face. She was beautiful and confident, but suddenly, she started falling all over the stage. The audience didn't know whether to clap or laugh. "Thank you, Lucy," Mrs. Linda said, with an embarrassing look on her face. "OK, last but not least, we have Taylor Nelson." Taylor came out in a beautiful gown. She walked the runway as if she'd been doing it all her life. She was perfect. Her smile and her body movement were all perfect. After Taylor finished, she took her place next to Lucy. "Thank you, girls. Please, give them a hand," Mrs. Linda said, as the girls all left the stage. "OK, up next is the talent search. This allows us to see what kind of talent is hiding behind all of that beauty. First on the list we have Marcie Henderson." Marcie came to the stage. Her act was comedy, she had the audience laughing at her crazy jokes.

10
CHAPTER

"**A**re you alright, Lucy?" Mickey asked backstage. "Do I look alright? Lucy snapped. "I can't believe that I fell on stage," Lucy admitted. "I know that Anna got something to do with this," Lucy said, with a fierce look on her face. Mickey pasted back and forth. "What do you plan on doing?" Mickey asked. I'm going to find out what planet she came from," Lucy replied. You're not making any sense," Mickey worried. "Mickey, I have a strong feeling that our friend Anna is not who she claims she is," Lucy said angrily.

"Taylor, you're on," Joan said. Taylor took a deep breath and walked out on stage. She was a little nervous, but then she looked at Anna and everything was OK. She had a peace come over her that she couldn't understand. She waved to her parents, that were sitting behind Anna and Brandy. The music began to play for her, and she began to sing. The audience was amazed at her beautiful voice. When she sang, it was as if she was talking to Anna in the song. Anna was touched by the song she sang. Tears began to pour down Anna's face. She was overwhelmed by Taylor's performance. Anna got up after Taylor finished the song and ran out. The audience all stood clapping for Taylor.

"Are you alright, Anna?" a voice behind her asked. It was Brandy.

Anna turned around with tears in her eyes. "No, Brandy, I'm not alright. How can I break Taylor's heart like this and tell her that I'm leaving?" "Taylor will understand the sacrifice you made for her," Brandy said, comforting Anna. "She may not believe you when you tell her the truth about you being an angel sent here to help her. But she will be alright, I'll make sure of it," Brandy said. "Thank you, Brandy, you are a true friend." "Yeah, well I guess I am." Brandy looked into Anna's eyes. "You know Anna, Taylor isn't the only one who's going to miss you." Brandy said, with tears in her eyes. "I'm going to miss you too." Anna grabbed Brandy in her arms and hugged her. "I love you, Anna," Brandy said running out. "How touching," a voice behind her said. It was Lucy. "I knew it was something weird about you, Anna. You come here with your perfect hair, your, perfect little body, and that annoying sweet attitude of yours."

"Lucy, what were you doing, spying on me are something," Anna asked. "Oh, I wouldn't call it spying. Spying is such an ugly word. I think it will be better if we call it gathering some information like a reporter or something like that." Lucy teased. "You see Anna, I got you right where I want you. I know that you had something to do with my little accident on stage. Now that wasn't very "angel-like," was it," Lucy mocked. "Lucy please stay out of this," Anna pleaded. "Stay out of what?" Lucy asked innocently. "I know you're planning to tell Taylor everything, but believe me that would be a big mistake," Anna said. "Tell me something Anna, why in the world should I listen to you?" "You don't have to listen to me Lucy, but for once in your life do the right thing." "No Anna, I'm going to tell Taylor everything," Lucy snapped. "Well then you leave me no choice but to do what I have to do," Anna said. "You don't scare me, Anna," Lucy stated.

"Very well Lucy, from this day forward, you will not be able to speak until you truly turn from your wicked ways and repent," Anna said, walking out.

Lucy arrived back, as the girls all formed a line on stage. They were asked different questions about modeling. When Lucy's turn came, Mrs. Linda asked her what she was going to do if she won the contest. Lucy stood proudly and began to speak. But when she opened her mouth, nothing came out. "Lucy, are you all right?" Mrs. Linda asked looking at her crazy. Lucy just looked at Anna and stormed off the stage. "OK, moving on," Mrs.

Linda said. "Taylor Nelson." Taylor stepped up wearing a beautiful dress. "Tell me Taylor, if you are picked as this year's model, what are some things that you will tell young girls that's trying to feel better about themselves?" Mrs. Linda asked. Taylor cleared her throat. "I will tell them that beauty starts from within, and not to lose their true beauty. To believe in their dreams and always stay true to God and to themselves." "Thank you, Taylor, for that wonderful answer. Well ladies and gentlemen, the judges are now putting their final votes in. Who will be this year's model." When Mrs. Linda said that all the girls walked down the runway for the last time.

"And now for the moment we've been waiting for. May I have the envelope please?" Mrs. Linda asked. "This year's model is no other than Taylor Nelson." Taylor just froze. Everyone stood clapping for Taylor. Tears fell from Taylor's face. "If my brother could see me now, he would be so happy," Taylor thought. Anna stood there clapping and smiling until she turned and saw Gabriel. Gabriel looked at the clock on the wall, letting Anna know that time was running out. Anna put her head down and walked out.

"Brandy where is, Anna?" Taylor asked, walking up. "I don't know she was just here," Brandy said, looking around. "Excuse me Taylor, they want you to come and take some pictures." Joan said. "I can't believe this Brandy, they are treating me like a celebrity," Taylor cried. "That's because you are a celebrity now," Brandy said, with a warm smile. Taylor hugged her friend. "I'll meet you at the dance," Brandy said, winking her eye. When Taylor went to take her first picture for the world to see, Super model Eliza Mikaelson was there to take a picture with her. "I can't believe it, you are Eliza Mikaelson," Taylor gushed. "Yes I am." Eliza said smiling. "OK girls I want you to hold these balloons and pretend you are just coming from a party." Taylor and Eliza did as the photographer said. Taylor couldn't believe it; it was her dream come true.

11
CHAPTER

At the dance, Brandy looked around wondering where Anna was. "Where are you, Anna?" Brandy said to herself. Lucy, Mickey, and Marcie walked in. "Oh boy," Brandy thought. "Brandy, I know what your friend Anna did to Lucy," Marcie began. "What are you talking about?" Brandy asked. "You know what I am talking about," Marcie said. "Anna did something to Lucy's voice." "What?!" Brandy asked. "Oh, don't play innocent with me, we all know Anna's little secret," Marcie fussed. "You see, Anna may have stopped Lucy from speaking but there is nothing wrong with her writing," Marcie continued. "So, since my good friend can't tell Taylor what a backstabbing, friend she got, I will," Marcie said, folding her arm. "You can't do that," Brandy snapped. "Oh yeah, watch me," Marcie said, getting ready to walk away. "Marcie please!" Brandy said, grabbing Marcie's arm. Marcie looked at Brandy like she was crazy. "If you don't get your hands off of me," Marcie snapped. "Sorry!" Brandy apologized. "If you do this Marcie, it is only going to hurt Taylor," Brandy said. "Do you actually think I care," Marcie said laughing. "No, I don't care. You see, you and your girls brought this on yourselves. Cheating to win the contest. No one cheated, Taylor won because she was the best," Brandy argued. "I don't think so," Marcie snapped. "You know, I wonder how Taylor would feel if she knew that all this time her dear precious friend was keeping something like this from her. Now, if you will excuse me, I have to find Taylor," Marcie said, walking away. Brandy stood there not sure of what to do. "I can't let her tell Taylor… not like this," she thought. "Anna where are you," Brandy said.

Anna sat at a church nearby. "My Adonai, I don't understand why it is so hard to say goodbye. I did everything you asked me, and yet I feel so lost. Adonai, I need to know why I'm hurting so bad," Anna cried.

At the dance, Taylor walked up to the escorts to see who she would spend her evening with. Caleb Anderson stood there thinking that Taylor was going to pick him, being that he was the most popular boy in school.

But Taylor wasn't looking for the most popular. Besides, when she looked at Caleb, all she could remember was being rejected by him. She wanted Justin Harp, because no matter what she looked like, he was always kind to her. She thought about the time when she dropped her lunch tray in front of everyone, and everyone began to laugh. But Justin came over and helped her pick everything up. Then she thought about the time she ran for class president, and Lucy embarrassed her in front of the whole school, but Justin encouraged her. Yes, he was there for her a lot. So, Taylor walked past Caleb and chose Justin. Caleb's mouth dropped open, at Taylor's rejection.

"May I have this dance?" Taylor asked. Justin looked surprised. Even he didn't think he stood a chance against Caleb. "Yes!" he said, grabbing her hand. They began dancing to every song that came on. They danced as if they were falling in love. "Excuse me Taylor, but I need to talk to you," a voice said, interrupting her and Justin's dance.

"What is this all about," Taylor said, walking into the bathroom. "I was in the middle of my dance," Taylor complained. "Well, this is more important than a stupid dance," Marcie snapped. "What is this about? Taylor asked again. "It's about you and the relationship that you have with Brandy and Anna." "I'm not about to discuss my relationships about my friends with you," Taylor said, walking away from her. Marcie grabbed Taylor's arm and yanked her around. "You are not leaving until I say what I got to say," Marcie said.

At the church, Anna sat there in tears waiting for an answer. Gabriel appeared behind her and put his hand on her shoulder. "Gabriel!" Anna said, looking around. "What are you doing here?" Anna asked. "I just came to see how my old friend was doing." Gabriel said. Anna smiled, and put her head down. "I'm not doing too good right now," Anna began. "It feels like I can't go on," Anna continued. "But you can," Gabriel said smiling. "You can and you will." Gabriel continued. "What is happening to me, Gabriel?" Anna asked. "You, Anna, are going through what so many other angels went through." Gabriel confessed. "What's that?" Anna asked. "You got attached to your assignment." "I don't know how, this never happened before," Anna said. "Well not every case is the same. You allowed yourself to take human form, Anna. And when you take on human form, you get all the emotions that comes with it. You experience life," Gabriel explained. Anna let out a sigh and buried her face in her hands. "I went through something like this myself," Gabriel confessed. "You?!" Anna asked. "Yes me! I was comforting this woman who lost her husband, and well I got a little attached to her. I mean she was a good friend." "What did you do?" Anna asked. "Anna, I had to say goodbye, and now you have to say goodbye."

Gabriel smiled and hugged Anna, but then his eyes got big. "Anna!" Gabriel said, pulling away. "What's wrong?" Anna asked. "There is trouble at the dance," Gabriel said, warning Anna.

"Marcie let go of my arm," Taylor snapped. "Ok, only if you promise not to walk out of that door and listen to what I have to say," Marcie protested. "Ok, what is so important?" Taylor asked. "Anna is leaving you," Marcie began. "What?" "It's true Taylor, Anna is not from this world," Marcie said. "You mean to tell me you interrupted my dance for this? Marcie, you have done some rotten things to me, but this stinks," Taylor said crying. "It's true Taylor," Marcie fussed. "Ok, you want me to believe that Anna is what, an alien from another planet or something?" Taylor said, folding her arms. "No Taylor, she's not an alien, she's an angel." Taylor looked at Marcie with tears streaming down her face.

Brandy looked around the dance hoping to find Anna. "Brandy!" Anna said, walking up behind her. "Anna where have you been, I've been looking everywhere for you," Brandy snapped. "Why, is everything Ok?" Anna asked. "No!" Brandy said. "Marcie is going to tell Taylor everything." "Oh no," Anna said, putting her hand over her mouth. "Taylor will be devastated." "I know, that's why you must tell her before Marcie does," Brandy said, worrying. Anna looked around the dance to see if she could see Taylor or Marcie. Just then she saw Justin looking around as if he was waiting for someone. "Justin!" Anna said, running up to him. "Have you seen Taylor or Marcie." "Yeah, Marcie wanted to talk to her about something. I think they went into the restroom…" Before Justin could get all his words out, Anna was already headed towards the restroom.

"You know that I'm not lying Taylor," Marcie continued. "What do you get out of telling me this Marcie? Do you find pleasure in hurting people?" Taylor asked. "No, Taylor, but you deserve to know what kind of friends you have. I mean Brandy and Anna should have told you," Marcie said.

"Brandy knew about this too. I can't believe this," Taylor said. She turned around so that Marcie wouldn't see the tears falling from her eyes. "I just can't believe this," Taylor cried.

Anna walked into the restroom. She looked at Marcie as if she wanted to strangle her. "Hey Taylor, if you don't believe me, why don't you ask your dear friend Anna," Marcie said smiling. Taylor turned around and saw Anna standing there with tears in her eyes. "Marcie, could you leave me and Taylor alone?" Anna asked. "No, Anna, I don't want to miss this for anything in the world," Marcie said smiling. There was complete silence in the room. They all just stared at each other. "Is it true, Anna?" Taylor asked, breaking the silence. "Taylor, I wish that I could talk to you when we're alone," Anna suggested. Taylor wasn't trying to hear anything but the truth. "Is it true, Anna? Are you an angel," Taylor asked again. "Yes!" Anna said, putting her head down. Taylor burst into tears and ran out. People at the dance all watched as Taylor ran out crying. "Taylor," Brandy said, stopping her. "Get out of my way, you backstabber," Taylor said, running out.

12
CHAPTER

arcie stood there with a smile on her face. "My work here is done," she said, patting herself on the back. She walked out of the restroom and ran into Brandy. "Well, if it isn't… but before she could get her words out Brandy punched her in the face. "You broke my nose," Marcie screamed. Brandy just stepped over her and went into the restroom. Anna sat there looking lost. "Are you alright?" Brandy asked. "No, Brandy. If you would've seen the look on Taylor's face," Anna said. "Believe me when I tell you I did see the look on her face," Brandy frowned. "What do we do now?" Brandy asked. "I want you to go home and wait for her to call, while I go looking for her," Anna said. "Ok!" Brandy said, hugging Anna. "This hug is in case I don't see you again," Brandy said, walking off.

Taylor sat at her brother's tombstone. She sat there and thought about that horrible night that put him there. "I wish you were here, Mike," Taylor cried. She sat there and talked to him as if he could hear her. "Tonight was supposed to have been the most important night of my life, but it was all ruined. Mike, I thought that I could trust Anna," Taylor cried. "You can trust me," Anna said, walking up. Taylor looked back at Anna and turned away and started to pout. "Taylor, you have to believe me when I tell you that I never meant to hurt you," Anna pleaded. "Why are you here, Anna?" Taylor asked. "I thought you would be long gone by now," Taylor continued. "I came to say goodbye," Anna said. "Just like that huh. After all we have been through together, you can just walk away like that," Taylor argued. "Taylor, it's not easy for me to say goodbye to you. This is the hardest thing that I've ever had to do," Anna confessed. "Well don't leave then," Taylor pleaded. "We can still be friends," Taylor cried. "I'm sorry Taylor but I have to leave. It's God's will, that I leave." "No, Anna, I won't let you leave. I can't make it without you," Taylor cried. "Yes, you can. You have to let me go Taylor and depend on God now more than ever," Anna said. Taylor turned her back to Anna. She let out a big sigh. "Go, Anna if you must," Taylor pouted. Taylor then turned around to discover that Anna was gone. Taylor wept bitterly. "Come back Anna, come back," Taylor cried.

Ten years later, Taylor sat in front of the TV eating popcorn. She was watching the first movie that she was starting in. "Come on Justin, the movie is about to start," Taylor fussed. "I'm coming honey, I just have to change Renee's shirt." Taylor smiled at her husband, as he made a fuss over their baby girl. "So, what did I miss?" Justin asked, putting his arms around his wife. "Nothing," Taylor said smiling. Just then, there was a knock on the door. Taylor and Justin both looked at each other and said at the same time. "Brandy!" "Come in," Taylor said, opening the door. "I'm sorry I'm late, but it was hard trying to get out of the office," Brandy explained. "I don't know why… when you're the boss," Taylor said, shaking her head. "I got bills to pay so I have to make a lot of business decisions. I mean everybody can't be a supermodel, slash actress and author like you," Brandy teased. "Hah hah," Taylor said, rolling her eyes. "So, what is the name of this movie you're starting in anyway?" Brandy asked. It's called "Lazarus," Justin said, before his wife could get it out. "Well come on Brandy, lets watch this movie because I have to get up and sign autographs for my books," Taylor fussed. "That's right, I forgot to tell you that I'm not going to be able to make it to the book shop tomorrow," Brandy said. "That's Okay! I'm just going to sign a few books and be up," Taylor admitted. "Besides, I had a feeling that you couldn't make it, so I put you a book to the side," Taylor said, handing Brandy a book. Brandy looked at the book and read the cover, "If They Only Knew" "Sounds like a good book," Brandy said, putting it in her bag. "What is the book about?" Brandy asked. "It's about angels being amongst us," Taylor said. "I can't wait to read it." "OK will you two quiet down, the movie is on," Justin complained. Taylor and Brandy looked at Justin like he was crazy, but then sat back and watched the movie.

The next day Taylor got up early and took a shower. After she was finished, she made her way to the kitchen. She could smell fresh coffee, and she began smiling. "That Justin sure knew how to get to a woman's heart," she thought. She made it to the kitchen and sat down with her baby girl. "Hey momma's baby," Taylor said, gently pinching Renee's cheek. "Ma, ma," Renee muttered. "Now why come you won't say Da, da," Justin said, looking disturbed. "That's because she's crazy about her mother," Taylor teased. "Yeah, well you better get out of here before you are late," Justin said, kissing his wife. Taylor grabbed her bag and some coffee and went over and kissed Renee. "Bye honey," she said, kissing Justin again. "Bye," he said. Taylor could hear Renee saying Ma, ma when she left. She just smiled and kept going.

At the bookshop she sat there signing autographs for her fans. The line was so long that Taylor wondered if she would ever get done. She didn't let that bother her though, she just kept signing books and talking to her fans.

Later that day, she looked up and saw that the line was gone. "Good," she thought, getting up. Just then a girl walked up to her. She looked to be about 18 years old. "Hi!" the girl said in a shy tone. "Hello," Taylor said to the girl. "May I have your autograph?" The girl asked. "Sure!" Taylor said, sitting down. "Who do I make this out to?" Taylor asked. "Anna," the girl said. Taylor looked at her with tears in her eyes. "What did you say?" Taylor asked. "My name is Anna," the girl repeated. Taylor looked at the girl again and then signed her book. The girl smiled, "I can't believe this, I got Taylor

Nelson Harp's autograph," she said. "I just want you to know Mrs. Harp that your book really touched me. At first, I use to think that I was the only one who thought that angels were real, but after reading your book, I'm convinced that they really do exist." Taylor couldn't believe it. There standing before her was this girl that reminded her of Anna, and not only did she remind her of Anna. The girl reminded Taylor of herself.

It was like Anna and Taylor's spirit was in this girl. It all made sense to Taylor now. "I have to give to her, what was given to me," Taylor thought. "Hey," Taylor said. "Would you like to go to lunch with me?" Taylor asked. "Really!" Anna asked. "Yes really," Taylor said smiling. "I can't believe this," Anna said excitedly. I'm having lunch with Taylor Nelson Harp. The girls at my school will never believe this," Anna continued. "You see they think that I'm a nerd at my school but wait tell they find out that Taylor Harp took me out for lunch." Taylor smiled at the girl, amazed that a few years ago, that was her. Taylor walked down the street with the girl and listened to everything that the girl had to say, as if every word that came out of her mouth was very important. Taylor smiled and thought, this must have been what it was like for Anna to listen to me.

THE END